THE GRUMPY OLD SAILOR

Janice Armstrong & Meilo So

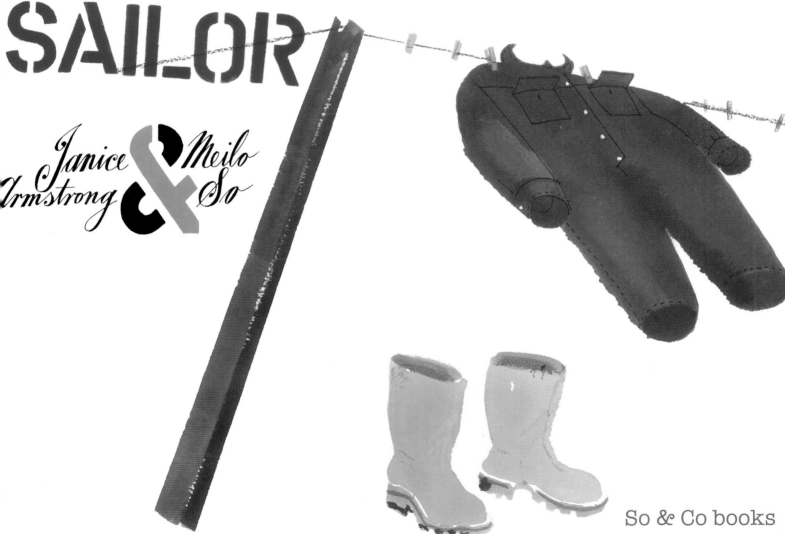

So & Co books

Text copyright 2010 by Janice Armstrong
Illustrations copyright 2010 by Meilo So
Published in the United Kingdom by
So & Co Books
www.bluemull.com

The Grumpy Old Sailor
ISBN 978-0-9563049-0-2

Produced In Hong Kong
By MI Design Ltd
January 2010
First Edition

One ice blue day
a kite
light as a tirrick
laced and looped
stitching sea to sky.
We four
danced the shore
leaping and laughing
passing the string.
I, Magnus
made that kite
painted the dragon's head
and tied a tail
a trail of ribbons bright.

Under the frosty sky
the old shore cottage stirred.
Men in boiler suits
tottered into
our secret house
with boxes piled high.
'Watch your step
you handless fools'
barks an old man
with a thunderous frown.

An old salt sailor
washed ashore
he cast a surly glance our way
then closed the door.

Like a stormy sea
all froth and spume
he raged
whipping the house
into ship-shape.
The roof tiles
filed into rows
glass gleamed
walls beamed
bright in the frosty light.
The little house
straightened up
the gate
snip-snapped shut.

The next day
we saw him
spricklin'
hither and thither
fingers raking the air.
A plastic bag
windblown bruck
had breached the border
between chaos
and order
teased and
tumbled and
landed in the alder.
He ranted
yelling at the bag
until
an old man
he crumpled
head in hands.

John Ross called
'I'll fetch it'
running to the gate.
'Oh no you don't
clear off,'
he growled
waving a gnarled fist.

Then there was the ball.
John Ross kicked it
hard
and it soared
over towards the
sailor's garden.
Exploding with wrath
he hurled it back
covered in kale
and curses.

A full moon
and with owl eyes
we went marching
in disguise.
With helmets and horns
and wooden swords
we went singing
up to his door
'What shall we do
with the Grumpy Sailor?
What shall we do
with the Grumpy Sailor?'

Then BANG!
the door explodes
and he roars
'GO
YOU PACK OF ROGUES!'
and in a
helter skelter
welter of screams
we scarpered.

As week rolled over week
we sometimes glimpsed
him working
making
scraping
swearing
planing
banging
sanding
sighing
pairing
sawing
building
something
and we
wondered
what?

John Ross the brave said
'A rocket.'
Vaila the sweet said
'A little house.'
Ingrid the strong said
'A tower.'
But I, Magnus said
'A boat.'

Once a whale
lay dead
on the shore
tide after tide
stripped it
white
to rib cage and bone.

Now a skeleton
of sweet smelling wood
curled out of the garden
and the sailor
hammered life into the
cradle of bones.

Flowering out
of the the frozen ground
a boat blossomed
the dragon's head
a lovely bud of red.
I, Magnus was right.

In mountainous clouds
a kite climbed
the arrow soared
toward the peak
and we skipped
faces uplifted
along the beach.

Calamity!
The kite kiltered down
a flaming arrow
aimed at the sailor
upon his ladder.

Bulls eye!
With a howl and a clatter
he fell
cursing heaven and hell
bucket and paint
went splatter
and the sailor
lay still
his violet eyes
wide to the sky
old man lying among
daffodils.

Would he rise?
We held our breaths.
At last slow and stiff
he rose
but did not roar.
His power gone he
gazed upon the dragon's head
and watched the paint
trickle from its
coal black eyes.
Then we ran
all but Vaila
who waited
silent and still
and later joined us
trailing the kite.

The next day
Ingrid saw him
limp from house to shed.
John Ross said
the boat was
quite a mess.
A tear rolled
down Vaila's cheek.
We all felt bad.

So when the stars
had settled into place
we climbed the garden wall
and set to work.
I chose the head
I know about dragons you see.
In silence
we painted and cleaned
mixing torchlight colours
following the sailor's lines
and as we worked
we wondered
what might lie
beneath the polished deck.
A chest of gold?
Or a bag of bones instead?

A curtain moved
and in the splinter
of light
I thought I saw him
watching.
Sure enough
the door opened
and he stood
against the golden light
and growled
'Are you coming on deck
or not?'

All aboard
the boat became the world
and we were travellers
from far and famous lands.
Hearts in mouths
we followed him
down below.

What a celebration
what a treasure trove
of a life.
Myriads of mementos
stacks of souvenirs
filled every nook and cranny.

From port to port
he led us
Dakar to Djibouti
Magadan to Manila
Ningbo to New York
San Jose to Sydney
the wealth of nations
filled each room
a glorious muddle
of cultures.

And so
we came to know
our not so grumpy sailor.
Days were spent
rustling and rummaging
in boxes and packaging
but mostly listening
to a life lived.

And what a life.
At times
we saw him sparkle
in youthful vigour
and then the tales
would like flotsam drift
and he would slip
into slumber.

The others smelling
salt air yawned
and left.
But I, Magnus
stayed
and laid a blanket over him.

Like otters at play
day rolled after day
Vaila, Ingrid and John Ross
came less
but I was
hungry to hear.
I silently mouthed
the strange
and lovely names
and played the stories
inside my head.

One evening
he handed me his telescope
'Keep it,' he said
'To gaze upon the world.'

The morning he left
we saw him push the boat
towards the shore.
He leaned with all his
strength
until gasping he fell
among seaweed and shell.

We ran
to help.
I, Magnus reached him first.
He looked up
his violet eyes gleaming
and in a whisper he said
'It's time for me to go.'

I felt my eyes sting
but smiling he said
'Nothing to fear
another adventure
another dream
to dream.'

Together
we all began to push.
It was strangely light
we only had to lean
and easily it slipped
into the glassy water.

Aboard
he gave the salute
and began to sing
'What shall we do
with the Grumpy Sailor?'
We laughed and waved
and the wind
did the rest.

I held the telescope
to my eye.
I had him framed
within a circle
and saw him dance
a joyful jig
and the dancing
raised him up
like crumpled paper
unfolding.
Amazed I watched
as gold seeped
through his hair
no old man now
but a sailor
in his prime
laughing
at the wind and sea
embracing all
bidding farewell to me.

I watched
until there was nothing
left
but the dark slate
line of the horizon
and a tirrick
flying over head.

Turning landward
once more
I saw the house.
The wind sliced
through the broken
windows.
A sheep
stood
careless
in the garden.

And I, Magnus
heard Vaila
cry
'Let's fly
the kite.'

To my mum & dad~ J.A
To Andrew~ M.S.

Glossary
bruck- A Shetland word for rubbish
kale- A type of coarse cabbage
kilter- "Out of kilter" means to be off balance
spricklin'- A Shetland word meaning scrambling clumsily
spume- Froth or foam blown from waves
tirrick- A Shetland name for the Arctic Tern